I Hate My Teddy Bear

While their mothers have tea, Brenda and John go outside to play with their teddy bears. They immediately become engaged in a game of one-upmanship.

"My teddy can count backwards," says John.

"So can mine," says Brenda.

In counterpoint to this foreground story are all the odd events that take place behind the children—movers transporting a giant plaster hand; a grown man wading in a pool with his model boat; dancers in 1920s costumes suddenly appearing on a terrace.

As *The Times Educational Supplement* said, "*I Hate My Teddy Bear* is a brilliant foray into the surreal—or, far more likely, a demonstration of the real: that the centre of any happening is never where we think."

A la Maria i la Matilde.

Clarion Books
Ticknor & Fields, a Houghton Mifflin Company

Copyright © 1982 by David McKee
First American edition 1984
Originally published in Great Britain in 1982 by Andersen Press Ltd.
All Rights reserved. Printed in Italy by Grafiche AZ, Verona.

10 9 8 7 6 5 4 3 2 1

Library of Congress Cataloging in Publication Data
McKee, David.
I hate my teddy bear.

Summary: While their owners try to prove to each
other which one is better, two teddy bears confide in
each other what they can and cannot do.

[1. Teddy bears—Fiction.   2. Toys—Fiction]
I. Title.
PZ7.M47866Iac   1984   [E]   83-7605
ISBN 0-89919-214-9

I Hate My Teddy Bear

David McKee

CLARION BOOKS

TICKNOR & FIELDS : A HOUGHTON MIFFLIN COMPANY

NEW YORK

On Thursday Brenda's mother came to visit John's mother.

Brenda came to play with John.

"Why don't you go outside and play with your teddy bears?"
said John's mother.

John and Brenda took their teddies outside.

"I hate my teddy bear," said John.

"I hate my teddy bear," said Brenda.

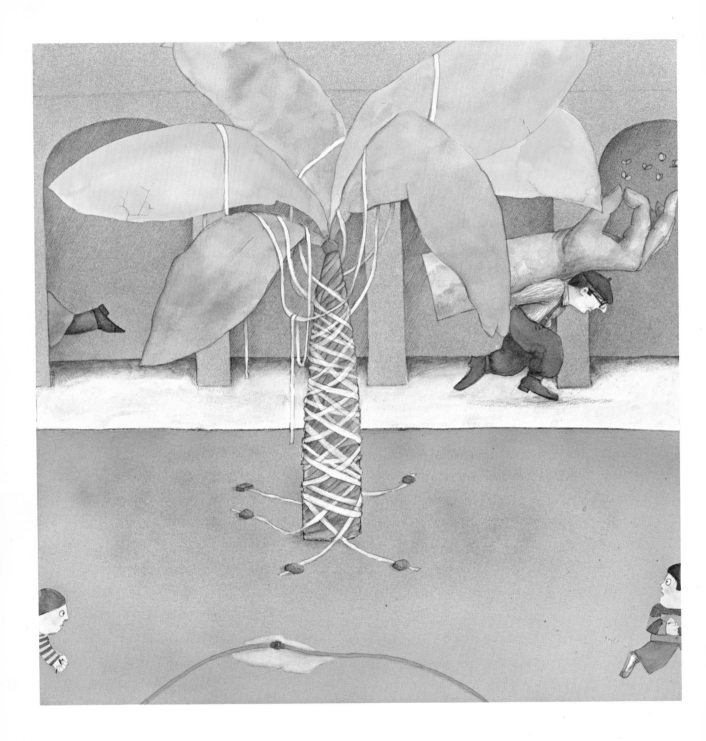

"But my teddy is better than yours," said John.

"No it isn't, my teddy's better than yours," said Brenda.

"My teddy can talk," said John.

"So can mine," said Brenda.

"My teddy can count," said John.

"So can mine," said Brenda.

"My teddy can count backwards," said John.

"So can mine," said Brenda.

"My teddy can SING," said John.

"So can MINE," said Brenda.

"MY TEDDY CAN FLY," shouted John.

"SO CAN MINE, SO CAN MINE," screamed Brenda.

"Teatime, children," called John's mother.

Before they went indoors, John and Brenda picked up their teddies.

"I didn't know you could count backwards," said Pink Teddy.

"I didn't know you could sing," said Blue Teddy.

"Oh yes," said Pink Teddy. "But I can't fly."

"Neither can I," said Blue Teddy.